BUGS
GALORE

Peter Stein

illustrated by **Bob Staake**

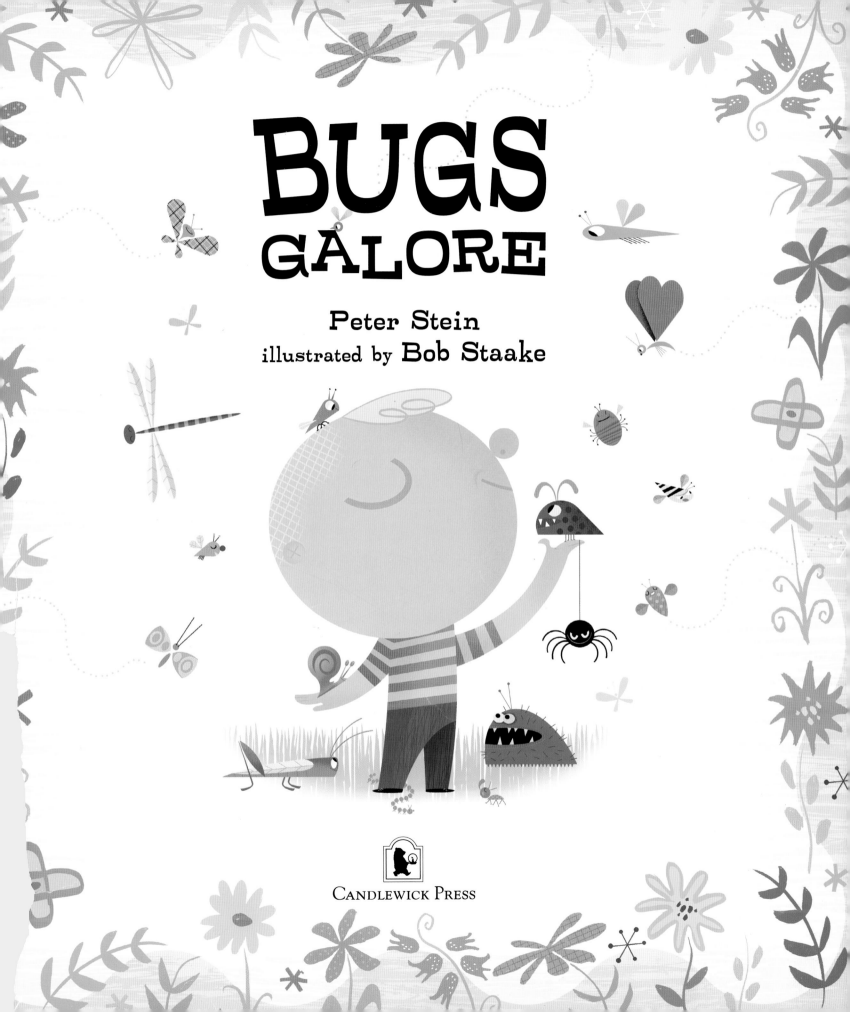

CANDLEWICK PRESS

Big bugs, small bugs,
creep bugs, crawl bugs.
Sky bugs, land bugs,
slime-your-hand bugs!

Dirt bugs, tree bugs,
hard-to-see bugs.
Mean bugs, kind bugs,
fun-to-find bugs.

Bugs and MORE bugs!
Can't ignore bugs.
Don't-inhale-them-
while-you-snore bugs!

Mud safari—
hunt for worms.
This one's squishy,
that one squirms.

Stuck-in-muck worm.
Half a YUCK worm!
Dig-down-deep-and-
find-with-luck worm.

Spider creeping . . .
scary. Gross.
Lurking . . . leaping!
Don't get close!

Freaky, sneaky,
shiny flat bug.
Hairy, scary—
what was THAT bug?

Honey-making,
buzzy bee bug.
Fuzzy, stinging,
time-to-flee bug!

Lightning glow bugs.
Nighttime show bugs.
Shining bright bugs.
What-a-sight bugs!

Some bugs cruise
around in groups.
Some bugs fly in
loop-de-loops.
Some bugs land
smack-dab in soups.

Some bugs crawl
right under . . . OOPS.

Blah! A stinkbug!
Plug-your-nose bug!
Funky, smelly,
wash-your-clothes bug!

Bugs and bugs and
billions MORE bugs!
Googols, gaggles,
bugs GALORE bugs!

Aaaah-bugs! Ewww-bugs!
Crawl-on-YOU bugs!
Stay away from
crawl-on-POO bugs!

Silly limb bug.
Swimming skim bug.
Frumpy plump bug.
Lumpy jump bug!

Caterpillar:
mighty changer,
body-morphing
rearranger.

Just like magic—
flapping, flailing . . .
butterfly-ing!
Soaring! Sailing!

Hurry, scurry—eating, speeding!

Hauling, sprawling—ANTS STAMPEDING!

Roly-poly,
snuggly ball bug.
Holy moly!
Ugly tall bug!

Love bugs. Shove bugs.
Head bugs. Bedbugs.
Cute bugs. Fruit bugs.
Live bugs. Dead bugs.

Bugs are awesome,
oddly mild,
feared and weird,
destructive, wild,
otherworldly,
pesky, chilling,
undercover,
fun and thrilling!

Bug, so secret,
are you wise?
Gazing out through
all those eyes?
What exactly
do you see?

I see you. . . .

Do you see me?

For Paul, Karen, and Nathaniel
P. S.

For Giambattista Bodoni—my type of guy
B. S.

Text copyright © 2012 by Peter Stein
Illustrations copyright © 2012 by Bob Staake

First edition 2012

Library of Congress Cataloging-in-Publication Data
Stein, Peter.
Bugs galore / Peter Stein ; illustrated by Bob Staake. —1st ed.
p. cm.
Summary: Bugs of all shapes, colors, and sizes—including bedbugs, cute bugs, live
bugs, and dead bugs—are presented in illustrations and rhyme.
ISBN 978-0-7636-4754-4
[1. Stories in rhyme. 2. Insects—Fiction.] I. Staake, Bob, date. ill. II. Title.
PZ8.3.S8193Bu 2012
[E]—dc22   2010047676

11 12 13 14 15 16 SCP 10 9 8 7 6 5 4 3 2 1

Printed in Humen, Dongguan, China

This book was typeset in Zalderdash.
The illustrations were created digitally.
Special thanks to Amelia Leonard for her buggy doodles.

Candlewick Press
99 Dover Street
Somerville, Massachusetts 02144

visit us at www.candlewick.com